Dedication

THIS BOOK IS DEDICATED TO ANYONE WHO HAS EVER HAD SOMEDTHING ON THEIR MIND, BUT COULD NEVER EXPRESS IT. ALSO, TO MY COLLEGE MENTOR/PROFESSOR/FRIEND, VERNELL BENNETT-FAIRS FOR BELIEVING IN ME, AND PUSHING ME TO TELL MY STORY.

I'VE GOT A LOT OF "____________" ON MY MIND!

BY

JAMES "TIM" DAVIS

Table of Contents

Excerpts from the play.....
"ON THE VERGE OF EXTINCTION"
Written by James T. Davis

MEN DON'T CRY

"ON THE VERGE OF EXTINCTION"

THE JOURNEY

The road you travel is not for the faint of heart,
This passage is for the more than conqueror,
and only for the set apart.

You go through far more
than the ones who counted you out,
Those who speak death on you, not realizing you are
more than what they talk about.

Your journey is different,
your steps ordered by God's divine plan.
You are more than a conqueror
because you never let lose His hand.

You face life head on,
even when it seems to be no end in sight,
But the faith planted on the inside
will not let you give up the fight.

Yet in your mind there are many battles
you feel you can't win,
But the fact you are still breathing, proves
God is with you until your journey ends.

You have feelings of loneliness,
and desolate you have also felt,
But you know God is the keeper of his word,
and you remember every promise kept.

Just know that as this journey continues,
you will sometimes think you are walking this path alone,
but never forget the one who will always be with you,
and who sits on the throne.

I know that what you are about to hear tonight
may be shocking and disturbing and
you may even be uncomfortable.

With our heads hung down with shame,
death knocked on the door of our lives.
Fear has engulfed our minds. We have settled for the
overpowering love that we know now to be abuse.
Hope became a faded memory.
True love became a distant past; abuse became our truth.

Now it is over.

We are tired of the abuse, tired of the lies,
and tired of being afraid of the perpetrator.
Freedom of mind, body, and soul, will come. We can't
leave here knowing that this may be our last time to ex-
pose the hidden secrets that are afflicting the souls of
many. We will be delivered from this
death sentence they call silence.

If the words you hear offend you, WE are not sorry.
We can't go another day, knowing that this
may be our last chance.

We need your help; we can't do this without you.
Don't judge us. We need your prayers,
your patience but most of all your love.

The secret's out, and the time has come. Many won't believe; many will not forgive. We have been afraid to talk about what today's community considers taboo.
We have been afraid to be who we are.

Man up! Stop crying! Stop being a Sissy!
You're acting like a bitch! Stop being soft!
You just need a good piece of ass.

Three out of seven males from the ages of 11 to 25 have attempted or have thought about suicide. We have ignored the signs. We have terminated the possibilities, and we have almost extinguished the ideal
of what a real man is.

What have we done? How did we let this happen?
Our jail houses are filled with casualties of our society, but worse our own community.

We have allowed our sons to be raised by mothers who have done their best. Yes, you teach us how to treat a woman, but you can not teach us how to be a man.

It has become the norm for fathers to be absent!

Instead of society celebrating the advancement on a job, graduations, and birthdays, we are just thankful that only one person was killed in the latest drive by.

Is it OK that our women
don't expect much from us?
Is it OK that our children
have accepted being fatherless?

It is time to wake up. It is time to listen.
It is time to take back our birthright!
How many more of us must die to the streets?

The door of communication is open, so that you will
know what obstacles we face on this journey
of becoming a man of worth.
If what you hear makes you think less of me,
then it is you who is holding me down
with a chokehold of judgment.

I must go on this journey with or without you.
When it is over, I hope you don't judge me
by how I look, or how I talk,
or even by who I fall in love with.

I have a secret….

Have you ever had a secret you wanted share,
But you didn't know if anyone would actually care?
Care enough to believe a delinquent child
labeled from adult chatter,
Felt thrown to the side, as if their life didn't matter.

I have a secret……….

Have you ever been in a crowd, but still felt isolated,
Many in numbers, but few to whom you were
associated…...with.
You share common places, common habits,
and even some common likes,
But your secret kept you trapped in a 24/7 night.

I have a secret………

Been told you're royalty and you bow to no one,
Yet the secret you've been holding has never been fun.
Didn't know love could produce so much pain,
Emotional, physical, and unbearable, longing
for heaven's gain.

I have a secret……

Most times you can't be
who you say you are in life,
Because fear grips your very being
and cuts through like a knife.
Stabbing through your curtain of defense,
this mask you call a smile,
The pain increases with every passing minute
and each traveled mile.

I have a secret.........
It's not easy to wake up
and put a mask on everyday,
Being happy, cheerful, and loving, always on display.
To show the world a fake truth as
you make your daily rounds,
Yet, your false truth determines
how fast you will drown.

I have a secret..........
As you laid your head to sleep,
You felt a hand rubbing down your sheet.
You prayed for death before you wake,
You prayed for the pain the Lord to take.

I have a secret..........
All you wanted to do was be a normal child.
From what the hell your secret caused is putting it….....
Mildly to say the least is a gift that will remain,
If your secret get's out
will your NEW dark place be that of shame?

I have a secret..........
Were you wrong to at first think love is what it was,
Not resisting or feeling wrong,
but letting it happen just because.
Because you never had anyone
LOVE you the way they did,
So you thought you were special
and maybe even their favorite kid.

I have a secret.........
It wasn't until your worst nightmare
opened your eyes,
Your reality of you being the golden child
was just a disguise.
Despite your efforts of trying to
please, obey, and hide the cries,
Your situation at the time would be
the beginning of your own demise.

I have a secret.........
Your best friend became a big white box,
It kept cold food in, and hot stuff out.
Loved you with what she had inside,
Never once were your requests from her denied.

I have a secret.........
Their "love" for you almost cost you your mind,
Following you into your adult life,
your emotions intertwined.
Tried to make sense of what you thought was your fault.
Thought in your head, the predators would remain uncaught.

I have a secret.........
Many years passed depression became your new best friend,
Accompanied by loneliness, and sleeping pills, the new trend.
Adult life hits different when you
have to live beyond the pain.
Wanting to kill all those who wronged you,
but what would that have gained.

I have a secret..........
The tears you shed tells the story of a victimized child,
Many details were left out to keep it mild.
You know many will ask, "why speak now?"
Because if you don't, another man will remain bound.

The secret is out!
God gave me the strength to speak for the ones with no voice,
But mainly for the child that had no choice.
I was positioned for such a time as this.
All the rumors of defeat, I want to dismiss

I am victorious!
Little did I know my story would be told to the masses,
This raw personal truth will not be found in your classes.
Who better to tell another you can live beyond your story.
Even in pain God's get the Glory.

I am alive!
Kept me alive to let men know it's ok to cry,
Forgive and trust God because HIS plan
was to keep you alive.
Many are suffering from a past that
was meant to take them out.
But now that you told your story, you realized you won the bout.

I am a survivor!
Yes my past almost killed me, not giving my future a
chance to live,
God loved me enough, so I chose to forgive.
Not for those who saw me as their prey,
But because I'm living in my truth and God has guided my way.

Where do I start? There is so much I want to tell you,
so many questions that I want to ask you.
I've done my best to make you proud of me.
I've treated Mama with respect and love.
I know that you think about me.
I know you are just waiting for the right time.
I understand, it's no hard feelings towards you.

Nah... I can't keep sitting here like it's OK
that I don't know you.
You think it was ok for my mother to suffer like she did
because she had to raise a son that needed his father!!
You abandoned me when I needed you the most.

Damn! Was I that worthless where you didn't
even want to know who I was?
Was it that damn painful for you to acknowledge
that you had a son?

I heard you are supposed to be a man of the cloth.
Do you realize the hell you put me through
by not being in my life?
Do you know how it feels to sit on Father's Day
and not even know what you look like?
Year after year, hearing "You take after your father,"
saying in my mind I don't give a damn about him.

I wouldn't have given anything to see the man that would
walk me through these doors
and rescued his troubled Child.

Damn, why dad? Why? Why the hell would you
leave me to the streets; initiating me into a life of
pure fucking misery! Why?!

Where you scared that looking into my eyes
will remind you of you?
I have to say that I love you even if we never meet.
I have never stopped loving you.
I forgive you for everything you missed in my life.
I forgive you. I just had to say this to you
before it was too late.
I hope these words float on the airways of forgiveness,
from that of a man that shares in their unspoken bond that will
reside in the heart of a fatherless son. **I love you dad.**

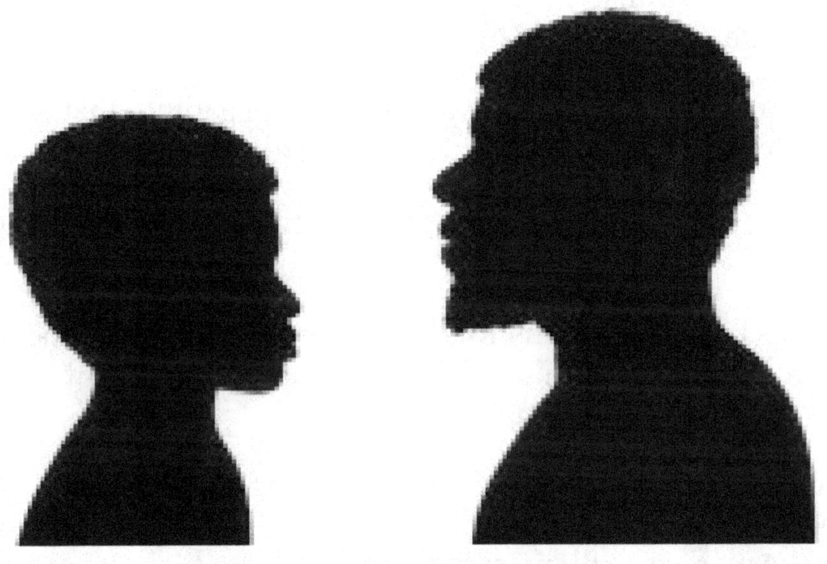

Hosea 14:3
"For in You the fatherless
find compassion."

Didn't know why I had to go through what I went through, but I thank you. I didn't know why I had to endure such pain, but I thank you. Lord, why I had to lose loved ones. Why I had to almost lose my own child. Why I wanted to leave this world, but Lord I thank you.

I thank you because you took me from a pit filled with damnation in fear. You placed my feet here: right here in the reality of forgiveness and spiritual healing.

 I didn't think that I would see another year, thank you.
I didn't know that these trials would lead me on my journey of becoming a man.

I became a man when I disposed of the negativity that had begun to set in like a virus into my very soul.

Lord you gave me life., you gave me worth, you gave me back to me!

I am a man because my love is not predicated on how people treat me. You made me from love. I have the blood of forgiveness running through my veins.

I became a man when I learned how to forgive you. Yes you, the one who tried to destroy my character. Yes you, who tried to use words to kill my spirit. Yes you, who took my most prized possession. **I FORGIVE YOU.**

And to you who said you loved me, but the only way you could show it was through the sporadic misplacement of your hands, which greeted my face often. I forgive you, because now, **I AM A MAN.**

SNATCHED FROM DEATH

I took a look in the mirror and saw a person
I could no longer seem to recognize.
I was a person that often used my smile
as a cover up and disguise.

Walking the earth depressed, defeated,
and living zombie-like.
Not caring about this world,
or even having the vigor to fight.

Often standing in a room full of people,
who claimed I would always be in their hearts,
But even that gave me no comfort, for my emotions and intro-
spections, were too many to sort.

At one of my lowest points,
hate had built a strong emotional barrier on the inside,
Having a heart of stone,
I felt my only way out was suicide.

The thoughts were so frequent,
that my mind became an internal hell,
Afraid to speak of my failed attempts to anyone,
out of fear of who they might tell.

My daily battle was the struggle
of surviving and wanting to stay alive,
Facing uncovered secrets and hurt,
that my smile could no longer hide.

Didn't have enough strength
to rediscover my own inner worth,
Even with that fact of knowing
I was called and chosen before my birth.

It wasn't until I gave myself permission
to let go and face the facts,
Accepting that God wanted to use
my testimony for a great impact.

I almost let my past kill me
for what someone else did.
Not realizing it took great strength to still live
beyond, even though I was just a kid

Don't know who this is for,
but I had to put forgiveness in the air,
And with the help of the Lord,
this testimony I was able to share.

Raised in church, but my peace a daily walk.
Some days I sit in silence,
and just allow God to talk.

I know I'm not the only one,
who God had to snatch from the hands of death.
But because of what He continues to save me from, I
will praise him with my last breath.

Excerpts from the play.....
"My past almost killed me"
Written by James T. Davis
SPEAK.

"My past almost killed me"

1) Break free momma

2) My past almost killed me

3) Taking it back

4) Addicted to the one I love

5) Did you even notice me

6) WARZONE

We learn a lot about Coretta Scott King, Rosa Parks, Betty Shabazz, Nefertiti, and Oprah Winfrey, but I never knew them personally. Now most of them are gone. All I have in life is you. But you can't help me because you have become a slave to abuse.

The World is changing, and more people are dying. The violence has become an epidemic, and women are being hurt!

In most churches, classrooms and households, there are many being abused. The worst part is that they are afraid to talk about it.

Why do you hide these crimes, these feelings, these heartaches?

The story has to be told!

It is time that you stand, and let people know that abuse has become the norm. Let them know they are not alone.

I know you think I'm not old enough to know, but even I can see that you have become a hostage in your own home. I need you to live. The only way you can live is to break free. The time is now Mama, tell your story! Tell your story!

From your 10 year old child

I took a look at my past and found that my past had my present on a string like a puppet.
Everything that I did, or was about to do, there was my past determining my next step.

I could not let anyone know that I wasn't perfect.
I could not let them know that I haven't got it together.
I could not let them know that I have a checkered past.
I could not let them know that I was one step away from letting the past kill the present, kill me, therefore not giving the future a chance to be birthed.

I didn't mean for this to happen, I didn't mean for it to get to this point, I didn't mean for it to bring me to the point of no return, and wanting to leave my education, my friends, my family, and my God behind.

I didn't know that it was wrong.
I didn't know any better.
I didn't know that it wasn't love until it was too late.
They made me feel loved. Like I was somebody. He made me feel safe. They held offices in the church. They were trusted by many. They weren't just anybody. You are supposed to obey those who have rule over you. You are supposed to obey your mother and your …….

It was my…….

I couldn't break the chains of guilt that had my mind bound. I couldn't forgive. I hated myself; I hated the world. So why go on? Why face this?! Nobody is going to believe me. Please, someone help me! Are you listening to me? Are you even there?

You said that you loved me, you said that I was your only one. I did what you told me to do. Try to be perfect. What is wrong with me?

Is my hair not straight enough? Is my waist not small enough? Am I not light enough?

Was my love not strong enough? You told me that you beat me because you love me. My own daddy used to say that. I know you don't mean to drink and beat me. It's me oh, it's not your fault!

Then I woke up.

I took a look into the mirror and saw the love he slapped across my face many times before, I looked at my back and saw the affection scars he left on my back, beating after beating.

I know he could change, but I wasn't being submissive like the bible told me to. As I cleaned the blood from the lips that questioned his whereabouts, I looked back to see my reflection, and I saw my mother, who raised me to fear God, but not fear man. Then I saw my grandmother, so my sister, I even saw my own child. Then looked one last time before taking my life, and saw that there were two visions looking back at me. I saw myself looking back, but I took another look and saw my destiny.

I saw a woman of virtue, I saw beauty and intelligence.
I even saw a glimpse of forgiveness.

I then turned around and took back my dignity,
Took, my joy, took my purpose.

I took back my life!

I gave back the guilt and shame!

My body craved you. I thought about you on the inside of me, and how you never cease to blow my mind. I begin to hunger for your comfort, your warmth through my veins... The way my lips felt after your touch, the smell of your essence will leave me in a daze.

You made me feel like I was your only love. Always took me to another place. Always there when I needed a fix to take me beyond my hurt, beyond my circumstances, beyond my hell.

What I didn't realize, was that you were trying to kill me. You became my conscience; stayed in my head. You became a part of my being.

I did not move or sleep without you. Would wake up thinking about you; go crazy waiting to feel you again. Withdrawal set in, when we were apart. You were my everything.

My family could not understand the love we shared. I gave up my church for you. I gave up my job for you. I lived on the streets with you. I left my family. My own child became an orphan because I let you get the best of me.

You were supposed to only be a temporary fix, and now I see you were out to destroy me. **But God!**
I was gone, no longer in this world. My own blood could not cleave me from your death grip. **But God!**
I lost everything I had! The death angel kept knocking on my door. **But God!**

God said, "Wait! You've been looking for love and now you have found me. You've been looking for joy, and now you've found me.

You've been looking for happiness, looking for life, and now you've found ME!"

DID YOU EVEN NOTICE ME ?

I would sit in church pews with my head down wondering if anyone would see that I was hurting, or that I was just trying to see who I wanted to sing at my funeral.

I was just wondering if any one of my Sunday school teachers would notice my best friend's depression and misery.

If my parents knew that my imaginary playmate they left me with was named Loneliness, would they still go to the church meeting without me?

My buddy Isolation would walk me to school every morning, constantly telling me I would die forgotten. Seclusion became my vacation spot.

I thought my job, my talent, my family will be the ones that bring me true happiness. I was wrong.

If you weren't pretty enough, you were forgotten. If you did not sing the best, you were forgotten. Even if what you had was needed at the time, soon after when you were no longer needed, you were forgotten.

I sat in church Sunday after Sunday hoping that the music would break long enough for someone to remember the name of a troubled child, or see the pain on my face. Maybe the usher that kept sitting me in the back of the church because I was not dressed right, but for a moment would ask me how I was doing.

Praying became distant. "God, you said you would not put no more on me than I can bear" or did the preacher make that up also? No one told me to fight. No one told me that they needed me. No one even knew my name until they were asked to silently read the obituary of our dear departed. Who decided that life had no meaning.

Love Thy Neighbor!

WAR ZONES

What has happened? What has happened to the world we live in today?

At one time they took prayer out of schools, and now my schools are no longer safe. Our neighborhoods are no longer considered to be villages of people raising each other's children.

They have instead become war zones, filled with casualties. We are watching our brothers being broken, watching our sisters being plagued with thoughts of unrealistic beauty, and watching our families being threatened by **EXTINCTION**. We have resulted in **DESTROYING** every character of our OWN people.

Have we become **our own worst enemy**?!

Instead of our young women learning how to be ladies from the mothers of the Church, they have turned to Tik Tok, Instagram and other social media platforms.

Instead of our young men looking to preachers, church deacons, and Sunday School teachers as role models, they have turned to hip hop, wanting to get rich or die trying, and in most cases many are just dying.

They have replaced Bibles with guns, candy stores with crack houses, and respect with death.

Funerals and visuals have replaced birthday parties and graduations. Some of our kids have just given up!

I stand here to let you know that it is time to take back what the enemy has stolen from us. Snatch back our neighborhoods from the death grip hold that drugs and violence have strangled us with. It is time to release the choke hold of destruction and save our village.

SPEAK LIFE
JOURNAL PAGES

Proverbs 18:10
The name of the LORD is a fortified tower;
the righteous run to it and are safe.

Speak Life

Psalm 9:9
The LORD is a refuge for the oppressed,
a stronghold in times of trouble.

Speak Life

1 Peter 5:7
Cast all your anxiety on him
because he cares for you.

Speak Life

____

____

____

____

____

____

____

____

____

Philippians 4:13
I can do all things
through him who strengthens me.

Speak Life

1 Chronicles 16:11
Look to the Lord and his strength;
seek his face always.

Speak Life

Isaiah 40:29
He gives strength to the weary
and increases the power of the weak.

* 9 7 9 8 7 5 5 5 1 6 6 7 9 *